*For Dad, who shared his love of science with me – KS*
*For Molly and Monty, who constantly try to defy gravity – AH*

First published by Allen & Unwin in 2022

Allen & Unwin
83 Alexander Street
Crows Nest NSW 2065
Australia
Phone: (61 2) 8425 0100
Email: info@allenandunwin.com
Web: www.allenandunwin.com

A catalogue record for this
book is available from the
National Library of Australia

ISBN 978 1 76052 661 0

For teaching resources, explore www.allenandunwin.com/resources/for-teachers

Illustration technique: digital artwork

Cover design by Andy Hardiman and Kirby Armstrong
Internal design by Kirby Armstrong
Set in 20 pt Archer
This book was printed in August 2021 by C&C Offset Printing Co. Ltd, China

1 3 5 7 9 10 8 6 4 2

www.katesimpsonbooks.com
www.andyhardiman.wordpress.com

# Ouch!

## TALES OF GRAVITY

Kate Simpson & Andy Hardiman

ALLEN&UNWIN

SYDNEY · MELBOURNE · AUCKLAND · LONDON

This is Isaac Newton.

People might tell you this is the
moment gravity was first discovered.

Ouch!

The truth is, people had been
discovering gravity long before Isaac.

ouch!

Ouch!

# Ouch!

# Ouch!

You might even have discovered gravity yourself.

Gravity's job is to pull things towards one another.
When both things are small, gravity doesn't really do
much at all. Which is lucky, because otherwise—

Let's just say it wouldn't be good.

When one of the things is **big**—

No, I mean **really big**—

No, I mean **really,**
**REALLY BIG—**

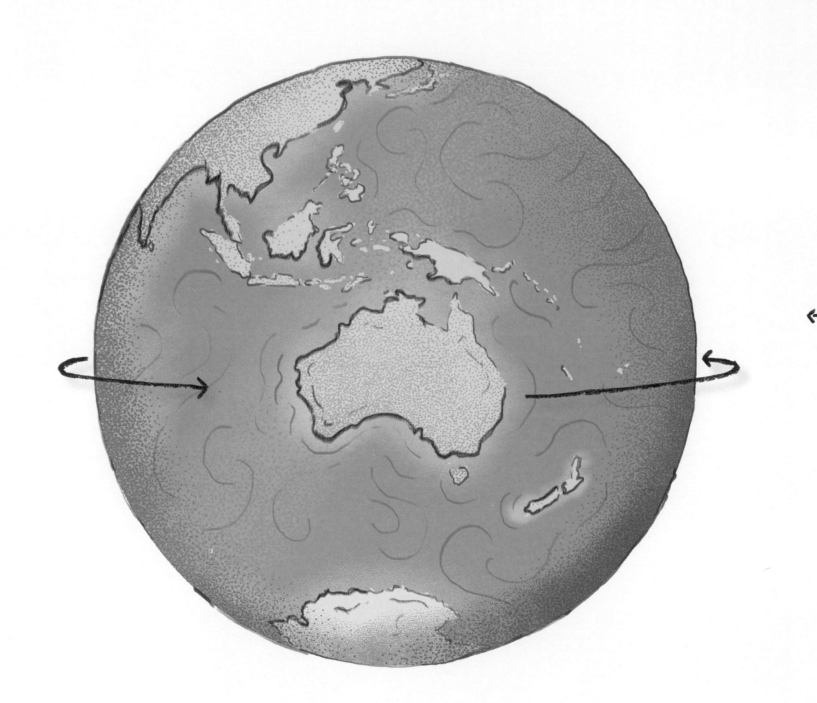

**That's more like it!**

When things are as **BIG**

as the Earth or the moon or the sun,

the *FORCE* of gravity

becomes strong enough for us to notice it's there.

Earth's gravity pulls everything down, towards the middle of the Earth, while the sun's gravity keeps all the planets circling around it.

Without the gravity of the sun, Earth would fly out into space, where it would get very dark and very cold very quickly.

GRAVITY

I think you'll agree we're better
off where we are.

The pulling power of gravity is what makes things heavy.

Feel this book. **How heavy is it?**

If you stood on the surface of the sun, this book would weigh about as much as a brick. **Why?**

It's because the **sun** is the most massive thing in our solar system. It's so big that more than a **million** planet Earths could fit inside it. Remember what I said about gravity working better when things are **big?**

Earth

To find out what life is like without gravity, we can pay a visit to the International Space Station. Because the space station is in constant freefall around the Earth, to the astronauts inside, it's as though gravity has been turned off.

Have you ever been in a lift that went down a bit too fast? Did you feel as if you were rising off the floor?

It's a bit like that.

Life without gravity
is pretty

# FUN...

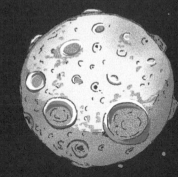

... but it's also a lot more
**complicated.**

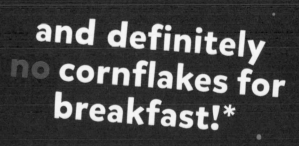

## and definitely no cornflakes for breakfast!*

*Also, if there was no gravity, the air we breathe would simply float away, which makes the cornflakes thing seem a bit less important, doesn't it?

For hundreds of years, humans have tried to **overcome gravity.**

And in recent times, we've had reason to feel
pretty pleased with ourselves.

But at the end of the day, gravity is the **force** that gave **birth to the stars.**

Come up against a force like that and there's always the risk of a little bit of—

# Facts
## about
# gravity

**Sir Isaac Newton** is one of history's most famous scientists. He lived 300 years ago.

Newton's ideas about gravity began when he watched an apple fall from a tree. He wondered why apples always fall straight to the ground. Why not fall sideways, or even upwards?

Newton realised that something must be *pulling* the apple to the ground. He wondered whether that 'something' would also pull on an object further away than the top of an apple tree. Would it pull on something as far away as the moon?

This was an exciting idea. Could the moon circling the Earth and an apple falling from a tree really be two examples of the same thing? Newton believed they were.

He imagined firing a cannon from the top of a mountain. The cannonball would fall to the ground. But what if he could find a higher mountain, and a more powerful cannon? The cannonball would travel further. If he could find a powerful enough cannon, then the cannonball would travel so far that as it fell, the spherical Earth would start to curve away beneath it. With the right speed, the ball would never reach the ground at all, but would continue falling around and around and around the Earth. It would be in orbit.

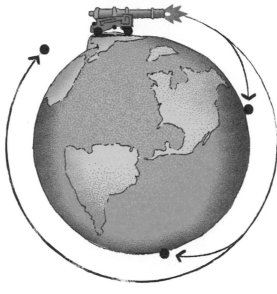

**Newton's orbital cannon**

For more than 200 years, everything we knew about gravity came from Newton's ideas.

Then in 1915, a scientist called **Albert Einstein** published a new theory about gravity. While Newton had described what gravity *does*, Einstein began to explain *how*.

Einstein realised that gravity is caused by massive objects bending the fabric of space and time, a bit like how you bend the fabric of a trampoline when you stand on it.

He also realised that as well as making things fall, gravity has another surprising effect – it slows down time. In fact, time runs slower when it is close to massive objects such as the Earth, compared to high in the air or in outer space, where gravity is not so strong.

These were incredible ideas about gravity. But they're not the end of the story!

Scientists today still have lots of questions about gravity that can't quite be explained by Newton's and Einstein's theories. People around the world are working to solve these mysteries, so that one day we can have an even better understanding of just how gravity works.

# Experiment with gravity

**Try this simple experiment to see gravity at work.
(Outside on the grass is the best place!)**

**1** Grab two plastic water bottles of a similar size.

**2** Fill one with water and close the lid tightly. Leave the other empty.

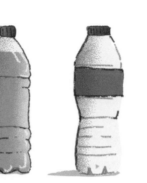

**3** Feel how heavy the bottles are. If you drop the two bottles at the same time, which do you think will hit the ground first?

**4** Drop the bottles and find out!

Did you see that the two bottles reached the ground at the same time?

Most people have seen a feather or a dandelion floating on the breeze, or watched a piece of paper fall slowly to the ground. It's easy to think that light objects fall more slowly under gravity than heavy objects, but scientists have shown this is not true.

A very light object such as a feather or a piece of paper will fall slowly because the air helps to hold it up. But most objects will fall at the same speed no matter how heavy they are. Even though gravity pulls harder on the heavier object, we also know that heavy objects are more difficult to move than lighter ones (try taking an elephant for a walk and you'll see what I mean!). The two effects cancel each other out, and the heavy object and the light one fall at the same speed.

In 1971, astronaut **David Scott** demonstrated these effects by dropping a hammer and a feather on the moon. Because there is no air on the moon to hold the feather up, the hammer and the feather hit the moon's surface at the same time. If you look on the internet, you can even see the video footage!

**Kate Simpson** is a picture book author, podcast host and bookworm who loves facts and fiction in equal measure. She is also a chemical engineer who believes that curiosity can change the world.

**Andy Hardiman** is an English-born creative living in Sydney. He has used his creative skills to design wallpaper, create gift cards, work in multiple advertising agencies and now illustrate his first picture book. He has a Masters of Art from the Royal College of Art, London.